Silas Marner

George Eliot

Abridged and adapted by Mark Falstein
Illustrated by Laurie Harden

A PACEMAKER CLASSIC

GLOBE FEARON EDUCATIONAL PUBLISHER
Upper Saddle River, New Jersey
www.globefearon.com

Project Editor: Ann Clarkson
Senior Editor: Lynn Kloss
Editorial Assistant: Daniel Heavener
Designer: Lisa Nuland
Production Editor: Alan Dalgleish
Composition: Phyllis Rosinsky
Illustrator: Laurie Harden

Printed in the United States of America
1 2 3 4 5 6 7 8 9 10 02 01 00 99 98

ISBN: 0-835-93584-1

GLOBE FEARON EDUCATIONAL PUBLISHER
Upper Saddle River, New Jersey
www.globefearon.com

Contents

Cast of Characters

Silas Marner	A weaver, living a lonely life after being falsely accused of robbery
Godfrey Cass	The eldest son of the wealthy Squire Cass
Dunstan Cass	Godfrey's younger brother, nicknamed Dunsey
Squire Cass	A wealthy landowner, father of Godfrey and Dunstan
Nancy Lammeter	Daughter of another wealthy landowner, wife of Godfrey
Priscilla Lammeter	Nancy's older sister
Eppie	A girl adopted by Silas Marner, biological daughter of Godfrey Cass and Molly Farren
Dolly Winthrop	A kindly village woman who helps Silas
Aaron Winthrop	Dolly's son
Molly Farren	The secret wife of Godfrey Cass
Mr. Dowlas	A blacksmith
Mr. Snell	Keeper of the Rainbow, a village inn
Mr. Macey	A tailor
Mr. Crackenthorp	A minister
Dr. Kimble	A pharmacist
Bryce	A friend of the Cass family who attempted to purchase Wildfire, Godfrey's horse
Wildfire	Godfrey's horse

1   A Stranger in Raveloe

Not long ago, spinning wheels hummed in quiet farmhouses. Certain small, quiet men lived far in the country in those days. They looked like a sad, lost people.

A shepherd's dog barked when these people appeared. They passed by bent under the weight of their bags. The shepherd knew that their bags held thread or cloth for their work. Still, he was not sure about the strangers' trade of weaving. He feared it was done with help from Satan.

Superstition followed any strange person or thing in those days. How could a man be known or trusted unless someone knew his father and mother? No one who came from distant lands was trusted. Any cleverness was seen as magic. Weavers were among the men who were treated as outsiders. They lived the lives of strange and lonely people.

In the early years of the eighteenth century, Silas Marner lived and worked as a weaver. His home was a small stone cottage. It was just outside the village of Raveloe. Near the cottage was an old stone pit that was no longer used.

The boys of Raveloe were half afraid of the loom Silas used to weave linen and cloth. They would look in through his window. Marner hated this. When he saw them, he would stare angrily at them. They would run away in terror. Who knew what those large brown eyes could do? There were stories that Silas could cure sickness—or cause it. In such places as Raveloe, people still believed in demons. They could not imagine any power such as healing that would be a force for good. One could only try to keep Silas's power from doing harm.

Raveloe lay in the center of England. The town was far from any main road. Ideas and beliefs from the outside world never reached the townspeople of Raveloe. Still, it was a good village with a fine, strong church. The nearby farms were successful.

This story begins 15 years after Silas Marner came to Raveloe. He was a pale young man with large brown eyes when he arrived. His appearance was strange to the people of Raveloe. This strangeness went along with the work he did. He also came from a strange land north of Raveloe.

Silas kept to himself. He invited no one into his house. He never strolled into the village to the Rainbow, a local pub. He wanted the company of no man or woman. He talked to people only when needed for his work or to get the simple things needed to live. Silas seemed to live as a dead man come to life.

Jem Rodney saw Silas leaning against a post one evening. Jem swore that Silas's eyes stared into the distance like a dead man's. His arms and legs were stiff. Jem feared the weaver was dead. But then, suddenly, Silas came all right again. He then said, "Good night," and walked away.

Some said Marner must have been in a "fit" that night. *Fit* was a word used for things that couldn't be explained. But some believed there might be such a thing as a man's soul coming loose from his body. That was how folks could learn things their neighbors didn't know. Where else did Master Marner get his knowledge of herbs—and of charms, too? He once cured Sally Oates of her heart trouble. He might have cured more folks if he had wanted to. Townspeople thought it was best to speak well to him. They hoped to keep him from doing harm with his "powers."

Still, Silas was a good weaver. He spent all of his time weaving cloth on his loom. He had no other concern in his life. The housewives sold him the yarn they spun. The richer ones bought the fine cloth that he made. His skill kept people from thinking badly of him. After 15 years, Raveloe men said the same things about him as they had at first. One thing only was added. It was that Master Marner had a lot of money hidden somewhere. He could buy up "bigger men" than himself.

Of course, Marner's life had a story of its own before Raveloe. He once had many friends. He had belonged to a small religion back in the north land. He was well thought of in his old life, which was lived in the town of Lantern Yard. Once, at a prayer meeting in his youth, he had fallen into a "fit." It was looked upon as a sign of God's favor by his friends. As for his knowledge of herbs, he had learned it from his mother.

Silas's best friend was another member of his church. His name was William Dane. William was also thought to be a good, religious man. Perhaps he was too proud of himself. William sometimes thought himself better than his teachers. To Silas, however, he was a man without faults.

Silas became engaged to a young servant woman in his church. Her name was Sarah. William would often join Silas and Sarah on their Sunday visits. One day, during one of their walks, Silas had one of his fits. William did not see Silas's fits as other church members did. To him, they looked like visits from Satan. Silas was not angry that William felt this way, only hurt. It also troubled him that Sarah seemed to cool to him after that particular Sunday walk.

Soon afterward, the church deacon fell seriously ill. Members of the church took turns looking after their religious leader. Silas and William often took their turns at night. One night, Silas was sitting at the old man's bedside. At one point during the night Silas realized that the deacon had died. It was clear that he had been dead for a long time. Silas couldn't understand how he hadn't noticed. It was four o'clock in the morning. He asked himself if he had fallen asleep or had had another fit. Why had William not come? Silas hurried out to get others from the church to attend to the deacon.

The next morning Silas went to work wondering what had happened to William. He didn't appear at Silas's house until later that day. William was with the church minister when he came to Silas's door. They had come to announce a robbery. Silas was told to come to Lantern Yard to answer robbery charges. Church money had been stolen from the deacon's bedroom. Silas's knife had been found in the drawer where the money was kept. They believed that Silas was responsible.

For some time, Silas could not speak. He was shocked. Then he told them, "God will clear me. I know nothing of this. Search my house. You will find only my own small savings. William Dane knows about it. I have had it for six months."

A search was made of Silas's home. The deacon's bag that had held the money was behind a chest of drawers in Silas's room. William begged Silas to confess.

"William, you have known me for nine years," Silas replied. "Have you ever known me to lie? God will clear me."

"Brother," said William, "how can I know your heart? Perhaps you have given yourself to Satan."

Silas suddenly felt hot. "I remember now," Silas said. "The knife wasn't in my pocket."

"I don't know what you mean," said William.

Silas looked at William but refused to say anything more. "God will clear me," he repeated.

Silas's church had its own form of justice. Members used to pray for a sign from God to find the guilty. They would pray. Then they would draw lots, or chips, to find out the truth. Members believed God would guide them to picking a chip that showed guilt or innocence. Silas prayed for the truth. God would prove his innocence.

The lots were picked, and Silas Marner was found guilty. He was ordered to return the money and to never return to the church.

"I last used that knife to cut a strap for you," Silas said to William. "I did not put it back in my pocket. You stole the money. You have plotted to lay this sin at my door. There is no just God of truth. There is only a God of lies."

William answered, "I leave our brothers to judge if this is the voice of Satan. I will pray for you, Silas."

Silas went home alone that day. He was so upset he would not even see Sarah. The next day, she sent him a letter. She was ending their engagement. A month later, Sarah married William Dane. Soon afterward, Silas left Lantern Yard.

Now he lived in a deep, wooded valley. The trees seemed to hide him from heaven. It could not have seemed more strange to Silas Marner. The God he had trusted seemed very far away.

Silas's first reaction to the shock of being rejected by his church had been to weave cloth at his loom. Each day in Raveloe, he worked far into the night. His weaving was automatic, like that of a spider. He hated all thoughts of the past. Silas felt no friendship or dislike for the people he found himself among in Raveloe. The future was dark.

Silas worked hard, and he was paid in gold. He had loved money little before. Every penny had its purpose in his old life. Now all purpose was gone. The habit of earning money became the only goal in his day.

There was a moment when he might have become closer to his neighbors. That was when he healed Sally Oates, the cobbler's wife. He saw that she suffered from the same heart disease his mother had had before she died. He remembered the herb his mother had used to ease her pain. His medicine worked. The news spread quickly through the town. People came to his cottage. They begged him to cure them or their children. They brought silver. Silas drove them away. He had no interest in earning money that way. He said he knew no charms or

8

cures. No one believed him. They thought he was evil for not helping. People blamed him for any sickness or accident that happened after he turned them down. The Raveloe people grew to fear Silas.

Silas began to collect and protect his money. He spent less and less, saving almost all that he made. He worked 16 hours every day. Each night, he would spend his time making piles out of his gold and silver coins. He watched the piles grow larger and larger. Every added coin made him want more. He counted them, felt them, and looked at them as often as he could. Silas's only love was his money.

He kept his money in two leather bags. To hide his treasure, Silas dug out a hiding place under his loom. He covered it with loose bricks to make it look like the rest of the floor.

Year after year, he lived alone, his gold increasing. His thoughts were always on his loom and his money. Everything of his old life had disappeared. The people of Raveloe called him "Old Master Marner," although he was not yet 40 years old.

After fifteen years in Raveloe, something happened in Silas's life. Near Christmas, a second great change came. His story became mixed in an unusual way with those of his neighbors.

2 Godfrey and Dunstan

The wealthiest man in Raveloe was Squire Cass. He lived in the Red House with the handsome stone steps. There were several others in the area who owned land, but only Cass had the title of Squire. The Osgoods were another old family, but only Squire Cass had tenants. He was like a lord of the manor.

The Squire's wife had died long ago. Perhaps this was why he spent more time in the parlor of the Rainbow than in his own. It may also be why his sons had turned out rather badly. They were not respected men in the community.

People shook their heads over the second son, Dunstan. Some called him Dunsey. He was known for drinking and betting. He was also a spiteful fellow. He seemed to enjoy his drink more when others had none.

It hadn't been decided if Mr. Godfrey, the oldest son, had turned out as badly as his brother. If he had, he would lose Miss Nancy Lammeter. Godfrey did not look half as young as he once had. It would be a fine change if Miss Nancy became mistress of the Red House.

Godfrey was standing in the dark parlor one late November afternoon. Dunsey entered. At once

Godfrey's face lost some of its sadness. Instead, it took on a look of hatred.

"Well, Mr. Godfrey, what do you want?" said Dunsey in a mocking tone. "You're my elder and my better. I had to come when you sent for me."

"This is what I want," Godfrey said angrily. "I want the rent money from Fowler to give to the Squire. Otherwise I have to tell him I gave it to you. He's threatening to take Fowler's goods for it. So, get the money, and quickly!"

"Oh!" said Dunsey, sneering in his brother's face. "Why don't you pay him yourself? I might decide to use this situation to get you thrown out of the house. I might tell the Squire you abandoned your child and left your addicted wife, Molly Farren. Then I'd slip into your place as comfortable as could be. But, you see, I won't do it. I'm too nice. You'll pay Father that hundred pounds for me—I know you will."

"How can I get it?" said Godfrey, shivering. "I haven't a shilling left. And it's a lie that you'd slip into my place. I can tell tales, too. Father would think himself well rid of you."

"Never mind," said Dunsey. "You'd like it much better if we both stayed home. You'll manage to get the money. If you can't borrow it, sell Wildfire."

"Yes, that's easy for you to say," said Godfrey. "I need the money now, and I don't want to sell such a fine horse."

"Well, you've only got to ride him to the hunt tomorrow. You'll get bids for that horse."

"Yes, and get home splashed to the chin. I'm going to Mrs. Osgood's birthday dance."

"Oho!" said Dunsey, trying to speak in a small, high voice. "And there's sweet Miss Nancy coming. And we shall dance with her and promise never to be naughty again—"

"Hold your tongue about Nancy, you fool!" said Godfrey, turning red.

"What for?" Dunsey replied. "You have a very good chance of marrying that fine young woman. Your wife, Molly, may take a drop too much opium some day and make a widower of you yet. Miss Nancy wouldn't mind being a second wife—if she didn't know it. And your brother will keep your secret because you'll do what he asks."

"If you had a little more sense, you might know that you may push a man too far." Godfrey was pale and shaking again. "I may tell the Squire myself. I should like to get you off my back. After all, he'll know sometime. Molly's threatening to come and tell him herself. So don't think your secrecy is worth so much. I'll tell father everything myself, and you may go to the devil."

Dunsey saw that he had gone too far with his threats. He calmly said, "As you please, but I'll have a drink of ale first."

"It's just like you to demand selling Wildfire," Godfrey said. "He's the last thing I have to call my own. He's also the best horse I've ever had. I believe you'd sell yourself, if only for the pleasure of making someone else feel as though he'd gotten a bad bargain."

"Yes, it's true," said Dunstan. "That's why I advise you to let *me* sell Wildfire. I'd get you 120 pounds for him, if I get you a penny."

"What, trust my horse to you?"

"As you please," said Dunstan. "It's you who has got to pay Fowler's money. You took it, and you told the Squire the debt wasn't paid. If you chose to give it to me, that was your business. If you don't want to pay it, it's all the same to me. But I'm willing to help you by selling the horse."

Godfrey was silent for a while. Then his fear won out over his rage. "You plan no trickery?" he demanded. "You'll sell the horse and give me the money? If you don't, everything will be ruined. Dunsey, you'll have less pleasure destroying my life when you know yours will be destroyed, too. And take care to stay sober. If you get thrown from the horse, Wildfire might get hurt."

"Make your tender heart easy," said Dunstan. "You've never known me to drink when there's a bargain to make."

With that, Dunstan slammed the door behind him. Godfrey was left alone to think about his life. He was

14

26 years old. For four years, he had courted Nancy Lammeter. She was a woman who made him think of a future with joy.

Yet Godfrey had made poor choices. His hope might not save him from a discovery that would destroy his dreams. If the ugly secret of his marriage got out, he would have to face his father's anger. Godfrey would lose Nancy forever.

What was he to do this evening to pass the time? He might as well go to the Rainbow. Everybody was there, and what else was there to do?

The next day, Dunstan set off in the cold, raw morning. He passed the Stone Pits on the way to the hunt. The muddy, red water stood high in the dark pits. Nearby stood the cottage where Silas Marner had lived for 15 years. Dunstan could hear the old fool's loom rattling. It reminded him that Marner had a lot of money hidden somewhere.

Why had he never thought to tell Godfrey to frighten or persuade the old miser into lending him money? Dunsey almost turned Wildfire toward home again but decided to go on. He didn't want to help Godfrey with this debt. Besides, he enjoyed having a horse to sell. The possibility of cheating someone out of his money was too exciting. So he rode on.

Bryce and Keating were at the hunt, as Dunstan was sure they would be.

"Heyday!" said Bryce, who had long had his eye

on Wildfire. "You're on your brother's horse today. How's that?"

"Oh, I've swapped with him," said Dunstan. It pleased him that Bryce knew he was lying. Bryce knew Dunstan wanted to sell the horse. After some discussion, Bryce bought the horse for 120 pounds. It was to be paid on the safe and sound delivery of Wildfire.

It did occur to Dunstan that it might be wise to give up the day's hunting and deliver the horse at once. However, he felt like taking it for a run. Dunstan jumped one fence too many and "staked" Wildfire on a fence. He himself escaped without injury. Poor Wildfire painfully panted his last breath.

Dunstan was glad no one had seen the accident. He was eager to get back to Raveloe without having to answer embarrassing questions. He began the walk back on the road near the Stone Pits. Mist was gathering in the air, and it was getting dark. He followed the light gleaming from Silas Marner's cottage to find his way.

Dunstan had been thinking about how he might get Marner to lend him money. He also thought the weaver might possibly have a lantern. He was tired of feeling his way in the rain and dark.

When Dunstan arrived at Marner's cottage, he knocked loudly on the door. All was silent in the cottage. He knocked again. He put his fingers to the latch hole to shake the door. To his surprise, the door opened. Marner was not there.

Where could he have gone on such an evening, with his door unlocked? Perhaps he had gone out for some reason and had fallen into the Stone Pits. This was an interesting idea to Dunstan. If the weaver was dead, who had the right to his money? Who would know that it was hidden? *Who would know that someone had taken it away?*

The question "Where is the money?" took hold of him. His eyes traveled eagerly over the floor. The bricks were sprinkled with sand. But not everywhere. There was one spot that was entirely covered with sand. The marks of fingers showed it had been carefully spread there. It was near Silas's loom. Dunstan lifted the bricks and found the object of his search—money! He had found Silas's bags of gold!

Dunstan gathered up the money. He quickly replaced the bricks and spread sand over them. Then Dunstan hurried out into the darkness. The rain and darkness had become thicker. He was glad of that, even though it was awkward walking with both hands filled. He stepped forward into the darkness.

3 Robbed!

When Dunstan left the cottage, Silas Marner was less than 100 yards away. He was plodding along from the village wearing a sack for a coat. His legs were tired, but his mind was at ease. He was looking forward to eating his supper. That piece of pork roasting on his fire had cost him nothing. It was a present from that most excellent woman, Priscilla Lammeter. Silas had today delivered to her house a fine piece of linen.

Earlier, as Silas prepared his dinner, he remembered that he needed a piece of fine twine for his work the next morning. So he had set out on an errand.

Silas felt it was not worth the bother to lock his door. What thief would be out in this weather, and why should one come tonight, when he had never come in 15 years? These thoughts were not clear in Silas's mind. They only explain why he was not worried about his gold.

He opened the door, glad that his errand was done. To his shortsighted eyes, everything was as he had left it. He walked around, putting away his things. Dunstan's footprints became mixed with his own. Then he sat down to the pleasures of cooking his meat and warming himself.

Silas thought it would be a while before he would finish his supper. He thought it would be pleasant to see his money while he ate his feast. He rose and placed the candle on the floor. He swept away the sand and removed the bricks.

The sight of the empty hole made his heart jump. The belief that the gold was gone, however, could not come at once. At first there was only terror. He passed his trembling hand all around the hole. Perhaps his eyes had deceived him. He held the candle over the hole, trembling more and more.

At last he shook so violently that he dropped the candle. He put his hands to his head and gave a wild scream. For a few minutes after, he stood without moving. Then he tottered to his loom. He sat down in the seat where he worked.

Now that the first shock of truth had passed, the idea of a thief began to present itself. A thief might be caught. The thought brought some new strength with it. He went to the door. As he opened it, the rain beat in on him. There were no footsteps to be tracked on such a night. Everything was just as he had left it. *Was* it a thief? Or had a cruel power left him with nothing for a second time in his life?

He drew back from that thought and fixed his mind again on the thief. Who among his neighbors had made suspicious remarks? There was Jem Rodney. He was a known poacher, who once had jokingly asked about Silas's money. That's it—Jem

Rodney was the man! He could be made to give back the money. Marner, however, did not want to punish the man. He only wanted his gold back.

Silas felt that he must go and announce his loss. The great people in the village would make Jem Rodney, or someone, give up the stolen money. Silas rushed out into the rain. He did not bother to close his door or cover his head. He ran until he was out of breath. He was at the edge of the village, near the Rainbow. The Inn, in Marner's view, was a place for rich and comfortable men. It was where he would find the important men of Raveloe.

Conversation was in a high state of excitement when Silas approached the Rainbow. The talk had passed from cattle to music to stories about the villagers. Now the men were arguing about ghosts. Mr. Dowlas, a blacksmith, did not believe in them and was proud of his position.

"I say you can stand out all night in your so-called haunted place and shall neither see lights nor hear noises," he said. "I'm ready to bet any man ten pound—"

"There's folks can't see ghosts, not even if the ghost stood as plain as a flagpole in front of them," interrupted the innkeeper, Mr. Snell.

"As if ghosts would want to be believed by one so ignorant!" said Mr. Macey, a tailor.

Yet the next moment, there seemed to be proof that ghosts were willing to show themselves. The pale, thin figure of Silas Marner was suddenly seen standing in the warm light of the door. He said nothing. He only looked at everyone with his strange eyes.

Every man turned at the same moment. No one had seen Silas come in. Even the blacksmith thought for a moment that he saw not Silas Marner, but a ghost.

At last the innkeeper spoke. "Master Marner," he said kindly, "what's your business here?"

"I've been robbed!" said Silas, gasping. "I want the constable and the judge and Squire Cass!"

"Lay hold of him, Jem Rodney," said the landlord. "He's off his head. He's wet through."

"Jem Rodney!" said Silas, raising his voice to a cry. "If it was you who stole my money, give it back. I won't set the constable on you. Give it back and I'll let you—I'll let you have a guinea."

"Me, stole your money!" said Jem angrily. "I'll toss this can at your eye for such talk!"

"Come, Master Marner," said Mr. Snell. He seized Marner by the shoulder. "If you've anything to tell us, show us you're in your right mind. Sit down and dry yourself, and speak straight."

Silas told his story. After many questions, it became clear that he really had been robbed. What was strange was that the robber had left no traces. He seemed to have known just when Silas would go away without locking his door. It was quite useless to set the constable after anyone.

"It isn't Jem Rodney who has done this, Master Marner," said the innkeeper. "He's been sitting here since before you left your house."

"Ay, ay," said Mr. Macey. "Let's not have no accusing of the innocent. That isn't the law."

Silas's memory was awakened by these words. It had been new to him this past hour to sit by a fire other than his own. It had been strange to air his trouble to his Raveloe neighbors.

"I was wrong to accuse you Jem Rodney," Silas said. "I don't accuse you. I won't accuse anybody, only—" He lifted his hands to his head and turned away in misery. "I try—I try to think where my money can be."

"How much money might there be in the bags, Master Marner?" asked the blacksmith.

"Two hundred and seventy-two pounds, twelve and sixpence," Silas said with a groan.

"Why, some tramp could have carried it away. And as for footprints, and the bricks and the sand being all right—why, your eyes have to be like an insect's. You have to look so close. You can't see much. I say that two people should go with you to Master Kench, the constable. Get him to name someone as his deputy. Then he can go back with you, Master Marner, and examine your place," suggested the blacksmith.

Mr. Dowlas and Mr. Macey agreed to go. Poor Silas, furnished with some drier old clothes, returned to the rain again. He thought of the long night hours ahead. He thought not as those who long for rest, but as those who expect to watch for the morning.

4 Where Is Dunsey?

Godfrey Cass returned from Mrs. Osgood's party at midnight. He was not surprised to learn that Dunsey had not come home. Perhaps he had not sold Wildfire, or had decided to spend that foggy night in the town of Batherley. Godfrey did not give his brother much thought. His mind was too full of Nancy Lammeter and of feeling sorry for himself.

The next day, everyone was talking about the robbery. Godfrey, too, was caught up in the news. A tinderbox had been found near the Stone Pits. It was not Silas's. The general feeling was that it had something to do with the robbery.

Mr. Snell remembered that a peddler had stopped in for a drink at the Rainbow about a month before. He had carried a tinderbox for lighting his pipe. Here, surely, was a clue. Memory can be fertile when joined with new facts. Mr. Snell now remembered that this man "had a look in his eye." He also had a dark, foreign look about him that showed little honesty.

Some disappointment was felt after Silas was questioned by the Squire and by the minister of the church, Mr. Crackenthorp. Silas remembered that the peddler had called at his door but had not entered the house. Still, he clutched at the idea that the peddler was the robber. It gave him a clear picture of where his gold was. He could see it inside the peddler's box. The villagers said that anybody but a "blind creature" like Marner would have seen the peddler prowling about. How else could he have left his tinderbox? Anyone could see that the weaver was half crazy.

Godfrey heard Mr. Snell questioning people in the Rainbow when he dropped by. He treated it lightly. Godfrey said he had bought a knife from the peddler. He had thought the peddler a merry, grinning fellow. It was nonsense, Godfrey said, about the man's evil looks.

Godfrey's interest in the robbery had faded by this time. He was worried about Dunstan and Wildfire. It would be like Dunstan to gamble away or otherwise waste the price of the horse. Godfrey set off for Batherley to look for him. On the way he met a rider. It was Bryce.

"Well, Mr. Godfrey, that's a lucky brother of yours, isn't he?"

"What do you mean?" asked Godfrey hastily.

"Why, hasn't he been home yet?" asked Bryce.

"No. What has happened? Be quick. What has he done with my horse?"

"Ah, I thought it was yours. He said you had swapped the animal with him. I made a bargain with Dunstan to buy the horse. And what does he do but fly at a hedge with stakes on top of it. The horse had been dead a good while when he was found. So Dunstan hasn't been home since, has he?"

"No," said Godfrey, "and he'd better keep away. What a fool I was! I might have known this would be the end of it!"

The two men parted, and Godfrey rode home slowly. He tried to imagine the scene of telling his father. There was no longer any escape from it. He must tell the truth. If not, Dunstan would confess it all out of spite when he came back.

There was one other thing he might do to win Dunstan's silence. Godfrey might tell his father that he himself had spent the rent Fowler paid him. Since Godfrey had never done such a thing, he might be forgiven.

"I don't pretend to be a good fellow," Godfrey told himself, "but I'm not a scoundrel. I won't say I've done what I would never have done."

All that day, Godfrey intended on telling the truth. He had to confess the truth about Molly and his child now. He might never have another chance. His father would learn about her in a far more horrible way—from Dunstan, or from Molly herself.

His father, the Squire, was known to make decisions in violent anger. He did not always care whether they were the proper decisions. He was not moved to change his decisions after his anger had cooled. Still, his father's pride might lead him to keep the marriage quiet. If he rejected his son, his family would be talked about for miles around.

By morning, however, Godfrey's will had weakened. He felt the old fear of disgrace, and of losing Nancy. It would be wiser to soften his father's anger against Dunsey. It would be better to keep things as they were. If Dunsey stayed away for a few days, everything might blow over.

The Squire was a tall, stout man of 60. He had a hard glance but a weak mouth. He was untidy, but he had a presence about him that was different from the ordinary farmers in the area. This was because he had always believed that his family and everything that was theirs was the oldest and best.

"There's been a cursed piece of ill luck with Wildfire," Godfrey began.

"What? Broke his knees? I thought you could ride better than that." The Squire spoke with a heavy cough. As he talked, he fed his dog enough bits of beef for a poor man's holiday dinner. "I never threw a horse down in my life. My father wouldn't have been so quick to buy me another! I'm as short of cash as a beggar. There's that damned Fowler, too. That lying scoundrel takes advantage of me. He owes me a hundred pounds."

"It's worse than breaking the horse's knees." Godfrey told his father about Dunstan, the horse, and the money that Fowler had paid him. The Squire stared at his son in amazement. "It's not a lie, sir," Godfrey said. "I wouldn't have spent it myself, but I was a fool and let Dunsey have it. I meant to pay it, whether he did or not."

"And what must you be letting him have my money for? Answer me that. You've been up to no good, and you're paying him not to tell."

"Why, sir, it was just something between me and Dunsey." Godfrey was not fond of lying. "It was just the foolishness of young men. It's not worth talking about. It wouldn't have mattered if I hadn't lost Wildfire. I'd have paid you the money."

"Foolishness! It's time you'd done with that. I'll not find money for your games any longer!"

"Well, sir, I've offered to take over the responsibility of managing things. But you always seemed to think I was trying to take your place."

"I know nothing of your offering," said the Squire. "I do know that a while ago you wanted to marry Lammeter's daughter. I didn't stand in your way, as some fathers would. Now I suppose you've changed your mind. You're a weak, shallow fellow. You take after your mother. The lass hasn't said she won't have you, has she?"

"There's no other woman I want to marry," Godfrey said, "but I don't think she will."

"Think? Haven't you the courage to ask her? Then let me make the offer for you."

"I'd rather let it be for now," said Godfrey. "I think she's a little offended by me right now. A man must manage these things for himself."

"Well manage it, then," the Squire shouted. "You shall ask her, that's all. I shall let you know I'm master here. Or you may leave and try to find an estate to live off of somewhere else. And sell that horse of Dunsey's and hand me the money. And if you know where he's sneaking off to, tell him to spare himself the journey of coming home."

Godfrey left the room. He was relieved that the discussion had ended without things being any worse for him. At the same time, he was uneasy. He had tangled himself in more lies.

5 A Kindly Visitor

Judge Malam was thought of in Raveloe as a man with a sharp mind. He would not neglect the clue of the tinderbox. There must be meaning to the clues found near Silas's cottage. A search was set for the peddler, but it was too late to find him. Weeks passed and the excitement over the robbery slowly ended.

Dunstan Cass's absence was hardly mentioned. Once before he had gone off for six weeks without a word. He simply came back and slipped into his old ways. This time, however, the Squire said he would not allow Dunsey to come in the house.

No one connected his disappearance with the robbery. His having killed Wildfire was enough to explain it. Godfrey assumed his brother was in some friendly place, living off of strangers. Godfrey expected Dunstan to come home soon enough to trouble him again.

Silas filled his loneliness by mourning for his gold. He still had his work, but his bright treasure was gone. Work brought Silas no joy. It only reminded him of his loss. His hope was too crushed for him to imagine growing a new treasure.

Yet Silas was not forgotten. His Raveloe neighbors now saw him in a new light. They had shunned him as a clever man who would not use his cleverness in a neighborly way. Now they felt he was not even clever enough to keep his own gold. His head was "all of a muddle." He wasn't mean or evil. He was only crazy.

The odor of Christmas cooking was on the wind. It was the season when people brought food to their neighbors. One Sunday, Mrs. Winthrop brought Silas some lard cakes. She took her little boy Aaron with her. Dolly Winthrop was a good, patient woman. She was always there to help when there was illness or death in a family. When she and her son arrived at the Stone Pits, they heard the mysterious sound of Silas's loom.

"It is as I thought," said Mrs. Winthrop, sadly. "He's weaving on the Lord's day."

They had to knock loudly before Silas heard them. When he did come to the door, however, he showed no impatience. Before his loss he would have had no time for strangers. Silas returned Dolly's greeting by moving a chair a few inches. It was a sign that she was to sit down on it.

"I was baking yesterday. The lard cakes turned out better than usual," Dolly said as she held out the cakes to Silas.

"Thank you—thank you kindly," he said. Silas looked very closely at them. It was the way he looked at everything with his bad eyes. All the while he was watched by the bright, wondering eyes of

Aaron. The boy was peering around from behind his mother's chair.

"But didn't you hear the church bells this morning, Master Marner?" Dolly asked. "I doubt you even know it's Sunday. Living alone here, you must lose your count of the days."

"Yes I did. I heard the bells," Silas said. The bells to him were a mere accident of the day. There had been no bells in his old life at Lantern Yard.

"Dear heart!" said Dolly. "But what a pity it is that you should work on Sunday. Now, Christmas day is coming. If you was to go to church and hear the singing, you'd be a better man."

"Nay, nay," he said. "I know nothing of church. I've never been to church."

"No!" said Dolly in a low tone. "Could it have been they had no church where you were born?"

"Oh, yes," said Silas, remembering. "There were many churches. It was a big town. But I knew nothing of them. I went to chapel."

Dolly was puzzled at this new word. She was afraid to ask anything further. Perhaps "chapel" was a wicked place. She paused before she spoke again.

"Well, Master Marner, it's never too late to turn over a new leaf. If you've never been to church, there's no telling the good it will do you."

Silas remained silent, not wanting to agree. But now little Aaron came around to his mother's side. Silas, as if seeing him for the first time, offered him a piece of lard cake. Aaron drew back a little. He rubbed his head against his mother's shoulder. Still, he thought the piece of cake was worth the risk of putting his hand out for it.

"We must be going home now," Dolly said, some time later. "I wish you good-bye, Master Marner. But I pray of you to leave off weaving on a Sunday. It's bad for the soul and body. Excuse me for being that free with you, Master Marner. I wish you well. Make your bow, Aaron."

Silas said, "Good-bye, and thank you kindly." He was relieved, however, when they had gone. Despite Dolly's advice, Silas spent his Christmas day alone. He ate his meat in sadness of heart. Toward evening, snow began to fall. He sat in grief all evening, pressing his head between his hands and moaning over his loss.

Nobody in the world but himself knew that he was the same Silas Marner who had once loved his fellow man and trusted in an unseen goodness. Even to himself, that past had become an almost forgotten memory.

But in Raveloe Village, the bells rang merrily. At Squire Cass's family party that day, no one missed Dunstan. The whole village was looking forward to the great dance at the Red House on New Year's Eve. Everyone would be there.

Godfrey Cass was looking forward to the dance with a foolish sense of longing. It made him half forget his old companion—Worry.

"Dunsey will be coming home soon," said Worry. "How will you keep him silent?"

"Oh, but he may not come before New Year's Eve," Godfrey said to himself. "I will dance with Nancy and get a kind look from her in spite of herself."

"But you need money," warned Worry in a louder voice. "How will you get it without selling your mother's diamond pin? And if you don't get it. . . ?"

"Well, something may happen to make things easier. At any rate, Nancy is coming."

"Yes, and what if your father should insist you give your reasons why you can't marry her?"

So Worry pestered Godfrey's thoughts in the noisy Christmas company. It refused to be silenced, even by much drinking.

6 New Year's Eve

Miss Nancy Lammeter sat on the horse behind her tall father. As they arrived at the Red House, she saw Mr. Godfrey Cass. He came forward to help her off. Nancy wished her sister Priscilla had arrived with them. Then she could have made Godfrey help Priscilla instead.

She had made it clear to Godfrey that she would not marry him. It was painful that he still paid her marked attention. Sometimes, he would take no notice of her for weeks. Then, suddenly, he was courting her again. It was plain he had no real love for her. Besides, there were the worrisome things people said about Godfrey. Did he believe that she could marry a man who led a bad life? Happily, the Squire came out just then. He greeted her father loudly.

As Nancy entered the house, Mrs. Kimble greeted her in the hall. She was the Squire's sister and the doctor's wife. On these great occasions, Mrs. Kimble was hostess at the Red House. Then Nancy exchanged greetings with her aunt, Mrs. Osgood, and went off to a bedroom to change. Soon Priscilla entered. This cheerful woman greeted her aunt and looked Nancy over from head to foot.

"What do you think of our gowns, Aunt Osgood?" Priscilla asked.

"Very handsome indeed," said Mrs. Osgood.

"Nancy never will wear anything unless I have one just like it. She wants us to look like sisters. But I'm five years older, and it makes me look yellow. For I am ugly—there's no denying that. But I don't mind! The pretty ones keep the men away from us."

The two Miss Lammeters walked into the parlor together. Nancy could not prevent an inward flutter of her heart when Mr. Godfrey Cass came toward her. His charm still affected Nancy. He led her to a seat between himself and Mr. Crackenthorp.

Godfrey avoided looking at Nancy while other men spoke pleasantly to her. The Squire was impatient at Godfrey's silence. Now Dr. Kimble skipped to Nancy's side. "Miss Nancy, you won't forget your promise?" he asked. "You're to save a dance for me, you know."

"Come, come, Kimble," said the Squire. "Give the young ones fair play. My son Godfrey will be wanting to fight you if you run off with Miss Nancy. He asked her for the first dance, I'm sure. Haven't you?" he said, looking at Godfrey.

Godfrey was uncomfortable. "No, I haven't yet. I hope she will, though—if someone hasn't asked before me."

"No, I've not engaged myself," said Nancy quietly. If Godfrey found any hope in this, he was mistaken, but she was not going to be rude.

"Then you don't mind dancing with me?" asked Godfrey.

"No, I don't mind," said Nancy, coldly.

"Ah, well, you're a lucky fellow, Godfrey," said Dr. Kimble.

Squire Cass called for the fiddler to come in. He began to play a tune, and couples formed for the dance. There were remarks about what a fine pair Godfrey and Nancy made. The other guests noticed when, after the dance, Godfrey led Nancy away to sit down.

But they had left the dance for a reason. The Squire had stepped on the bottom of Nancy's dress. This had caused some stitches to tear. Nancy exchanged a glance and a whisper with Priscilla. She said to Godfrey that she must sit down until her sister could come to her. Godfrey was feeling so happy about being with Nancy that he went with her without being asked. He led her into a small parlor where card tables were set up.

Nancy said coldly, "I'll wait here alone until my sister comes. I need not give you any more trouble. I'm sorry you've had such an unlucky partner."

"You know that isn't true," said Godfrey as he sat down. "You know one dance with you matters more to me than all the pleasures in the world."

It had been a long time since Godfrey had spoken to her like this. He had been withdrawn for

sometime. Nancy was startled, but she would not let her feelings show.

"No, indeed, Mr. Godfrey, that's not known to me. I have good reasons for thinking different. But even if it's true, I don't wish to hear it."

"Would you never forgive me then, Nancy? Can you never think well of me? Can't the present ever make up for the past—not even if I change?"

Godfrey was aware that his feelings had gotten the better of his tongue. Nancy was much disturbed by what his words suggested. She roused all her power of self-command.

"I'd feel glad to see a good change in anybody, Mr. Godfrey," she said. "But it would be better if no change was needed."

Godfrey would have liked to go on, but just then Priscilla hurried into the room. "Dear heart, child, let us look at this gown!" she said.

"I suppose I must go now," Godfrey said.

"As you like," said Nancy, trying to keep her coldness.

"Then I like to stay," said Godfrey. He wanted to get as much joy as he could tonight and think nothing of tomorrow.

7   Gold on the Hearth

While Godfrey was enjoying Nancy's sweet presence, his wife Molly was walking slowly toward Raveloe. She was carrying their child in her arms.

This journey was an act of revenge. Godfrey had said he would sooner die than acknowledge her as his wife. Molly knew there would be a great party at the Red House on New Year's Eve. Her husband would be smiling and smiled upon. Molly decided she would ruin his pleasure. She would go in her dirty rags, holding their child. She would show herself to the Squire as his eldest son's wife.

People who are miserable usually see their misery as a wrong done to them by someone else. Molly knew that her misery was not only her husband's fault. She was a slave to a demon—Opium. Yet she was bitter toward Godfrey. *He* was well off. If she had her rights, she would be well off, too.

She had started early but had taken too long on the road. Now, near Raveloe, a freezing wind had come up. She needed comfort. She turned to the opium in her pocket. She took out the liquid and drank. She threw the empty bottle away. Then she walked on, growing ever more sleepy. She clutched the sleeping child closer to her chest.

Slowly, the opium worked its will on Molly's body and mind. Cold and weariness were its helpers. She sank down against a bush. She could walk no further. The bed of snow was soft. She did not feel the cold. The little one slept on gently in her arms.

At last Molly fell asleep. Her hold on the child relaxed. The little head fell away from her chest. The child's blue eyes opened wide. There was a cry of "Mammy!" But its Mother's ears were deaf.

The child rolled down its mother's knees, all wet with snow. Its eyes caught a bright light on the white ground. The child reached out a little hand to catch the gleam. Her head lifted up to see where the light came from. It came from a very bright place.

The child rose on its legs. It toddled through the snow—to the open door of Silas Marner's cottage. It went right up to the warm hearth. A bright fire was warming the old sack that was Silas's coat. The little one was used to being left alone. It lay down and spread its tiny hands toward the cheerful fire. Soon the blue eyes were closed.

But where was Silas Marner? He was in the cottage, but he did not see the child. Silas stood frozen at the door in one of his fits. He often opened his door and looked out. It was as though he thought he might see his money coming back.

That morning, some of his neighbors had told him it was good luck to sit up and listen to the New Year being rung in. It might bring his money back. This was just a friendly Raveloe way of joking with the crazy old miser. That night when Silas opened his door, he fell into one his spells. He stood like a statue, holding open the door.

When his senses returned, he closed the door. The light had grown dim. He was chilled and weak. He turned toward the hearth and sat down on the chair by the fire. He bent to push the logs together. Then, to his hazy sight, it seemed as if there were gold in front of the hearth. Gold—his own gold—brought back to him as mysteriously as it had been taken away!

His heart began to beat violently. He leaned forward and stretched out his hand. Instead of hard coins, his fingers touched soft, warm curls. Amazed, Silas fell on his knees. He bent forward to examine the wonder more closely. It was a sleeping child. Could this be his little sister come back in a dream? Could it be the sister he had carried in his arms for a year, who had died when he was a boy?

Silas rose to his feet. He built up the fire. The flame did not make the vision disappear. How and when had the child come in?

There was a cry on the hearth. The child had awakened. Marner bent to pick it up. It hugged his neck and burst into loud cries of "Mammy." Silas held it and made sounds of hushing tenderness.

He had plenty to do in the next hour. He fed the child hot cereal sweetened with brown sugar. The

43

cereal stopped the little one's cries. She lifted her blue eyes with a wide, quiet gaze at Silas.

Soon the golden child began to toddle about the cottage. Silas followed her to keep her from falling against anything that could hurt her. She sat on the ground and began to pull at her boots. She looked up at him, crying softly. It occurred to Silas that the boots were wet. He got them off, and the baby became happily involved in her own toes.

The wet boots suggested to Silas that the baby had been walking in the snow. He lifted the child in his arms. As soon as he had opened the door, there was the cry of "Mammy" again. He could see the marks made by the little feet in the snow. He followed the tracks to the bushes. "Mammy!" the little one called again. It stretched forward and almost escaped from Silas's arms. It was then that he saw that there was something more than a bush before him. There was a human body, half covered with snow.

Suppertime at the Red House had ended. The mood had passed into easy laughter. The servants' heavy duties were over. They were getting their share of amusement by watching the dancing.

Godfrey's other brother Bob Cass was doing a lively dance. Godfrey was standing a little way off. He was watching Nancy. She was seated in a group near her father. Suddenly, Godfrey lifted his eyes. He saw something as startling as if it had been a ghost. It was his own child, being carried in Silas Marner's arms.

Mr. Crackenthorp and Mr. Lammeter approached Silas. Godfrey joined them, needing to hear every word. He knew that if anyone noticed him, they would see that he was pale and trembling.

The Squire himself had risen. He asked angrily, "What do you mean coming in here this way?"

"I've come for the doctor," said Silas.

"Why, what's the matter, Marner?" asked Mr. Crackenthorp. "The doctor's here, but say quietly what you want him for."

"It's a woman," Silas said, speaking low. "She's dead, I think—in the snow near my house."

Godfrey felt a great terror at that moment—the woman might *not* be dead. Such thoughts can enter even a kind heart if its happiness depends on lies.

Mr. Crackenthorp sent someone to find Dr. Kimble. By then the ladies had pressed forward. They were curious to know why the weaver was there. They were also interested in the pretty child, who frowned and hid her face.

"What child is it?" said Nancy Lammeter. She was speaking to Godfrey.

"I don't know. Some poor woman's who has been found in the snow, I believe." Godfrey pulled the answer from himself with a terrible effort.

"Why, you'd better leave the child here then, Master Marner," said Mrs. Kimble. "I'll tell one of the girls to fetch it."

"No. I can't part with it. I can't let it go," said Silas.

"It's come to me. I've a right to keep it."

His own words surprised Silas. Just before, he'd had no clear thought about keeping the child.

"Did you ever hear of such a thing?" said Mrs. Kimble, in mild surprise, to her neighbor.

Dr. Kimble came in from the card room. He hurried out with Marner. They were followed by Godfrey and Mr. Crackenthorp.

"Get me a pair of thick boots, Godfrey, will you?" Dr. Kimble asked. "And let somebody go to Winthrop's and fetch Dolly. She's the best woman to get."

The child had begun to cry and call for "Mammy," though she held tightly to Marner. Godfrey felt the cry as if some thread were pulled tight inside him. In a few minutes, Silas and the men from Red House were on their way back to the Stone Pits.

"Is she dead?" said the voice within Godfrey. "If she is, I may marry Nancy. I will be a good fellow in the future. And the child—she shall be taken care of somehow." But then there came another thought. "She may live—and then it's all over for me."

Godfrey didn't know how long it was before the cottage door opened and Mr. Kimble came out. The doctor had been examining the woman inside the cottage. She had been moved inside earlier.

"There's nothing to be done," he said. "She's dead—been dead for hours, I should say. A very thin young woman. Homeless—quite in rags. She's got a wedding ring on, though."

"I want to look at her," said Godfrey.

Godfrey went into the cottage. He glanced at the dead face on the pillow. He would well remember that last look on his unhappy, hated wife.

He turned toward the hearth, where Silas sat calming the child. "You'll take the child to the church tomorrow?" Godfrey asked casually.

"Who says so?" asked Marner sharply. "Will they make me?"

"Why, you wouldn't like to keep her, would you?" asked Godfrey. "An old bachelor like you?"

"I'll keep her till anyone shows me they have a right to take her away," said Marner. "The mother's dead, and I reckon it's got no father. It's a lone thing; I'm a lone thing. My money's gone. This has come from I don't know where."

"Poor little thing!" said Godfrey. "Let me give something toward finding it clothes." He put his hand in his pocket and found half a guinea. He thrust it into Silas's hand and hurried outside.

Godfrey returned to the party with a sense of relief and gladness. Could he not now promise Nancy all that she wanted of him? His marriage to Molly would never be discovered.

What would be the use in telling Nancy the truth? As for the child, he would see that it was cared for. He would do everything but own it. Perhaps it would be just as happy that way. Who could tell?

8 Eppie

There was a pauper's burial in Raveloe for Molly that week. In Batherley, it was known that the dark-haired woman who had been staying there with her child had gone away. That was the only note taken of Molly's disappearance.

Silas's keeping the child was talked about as much as the robbery of his money. People now felt sympathy for him, especially the women. Mothers were ready with their advice. The good ones told him what he had better do to care for the child. The lazy ones told him what he would never be able to do.

Of all of the mothers, Dolly Winthrop was the one whose advice was most welcomed. Silas had shown her the money given to him by Godfrey to buy clothes for the child.

"Eh, Master Marner," said Dolly, "there's no call to buy more than a pair of shoes. I've got the clothes Aaron wore five years ago. It's no use spending money on baby clothes. That child will grow like grass in May. Bless it, that it will."

"The angels in heaven couldn't be prettier," Dolly said. She then rubbed the girl's hair and kissed it. "I think you're right to keep it, Master Marner. It's been sent to you. You'll be a bit troubled with it while it's so little. I'll come by and help you. I've a bit of time to spare most days."

"Thank you . . . kindly," Silas said. "I'll be glad if you tell me things. But I want to do things for myself. Else it might get fond of someone else, and not of me. I've been used to doing for myself. I can learn. I can learn."

"Eh, to be sure," Dolly said gently.

Marner took the child on his lap. He was trembling with a strange feeling. Something new was beginning in his life. It was as if the gold had turned into the child.

"There, then. Why, you take to it quite easy," Dolly said. "But what will you do when you must work at your loom?"

"I'll tie her to the leg of the loom," Silas said. "Tie her with a long strip of something."

"Well, perhaps that will do. But I'll bring you my little chair, and some things for her to play with. I can teach her to clean, mend, and knit when she gets old enough."

"But she'll be *my* little one," Marner said. "She'll be no one else's."

"No, to be sure, if you're a father to her," said Dolly. "But you must bring her up like christened folks' children. You must take her to church."

Dolly was silent for some time. She was eager and concerned to know how her words would be taken by Silas. He was puzzled and worried. Dolly's word "christened" had no clear meaning for him.

"What do you mean by 'christened'?" he asked. "Won't folks be good to her without it?"

"Dear, dear, Master Marner," said Dolly. "Had you no father or mother who taught you prayers?"

"Yes," said Silas, in a low voice. "I know about that—used to. But your ways are different." He paused for a few moments. "But whatever is right for the child in this country, I'll do."

"Well, then, Mr. Marner, I'll speak to the parson about it. And you decide on a name for the child. It must have a name given it when it's christened."

"My little sister's name was Hephzibah," Silas said. "It's a Bible name."

"Then I have no call to speak against it," said Dolly. She was startled by Silas's knowledge of the Bible. "But it was hard calling your little sister by such a big name, wasn't it, Master Marner?"

"We called her Eppie," said Silas.

"Well, that would be handier. And so I'll go now, Master Marner. I'll speak of the christening before dark. I wish you the best of luck. It's my belief it will come to you, if you do right by the child," said Dunlap.

The baby *was* christened. Silas appeared for the first time in church. He had no clear idea about going to church, except that Dolly said it was for the good of the child. In this way, as time passed, the

child created new links between Silas and his neighbors.

His gold had needed nothing. It had to be worshipped in solitude, hidden from daylight.

Eppie was a creature of endless needs and desires. In the past, the gold had kept his thoughts constant. In Silas's old life each day was the same as the last. The child changed everything. Eppie was made of changes and hopes that drove his thoughts onward. The gold had kept him at his weaving. Eppie called him away from his weaving. She made all pauses seem like a holiday. She reawakened his senses with her fresh life. She warmed him into joy because *she* had joy.

Silas would carry her beyond the Stone Pits to the meadow where flowers grew. Eppie would pick flowers for "Dad-dad" and talk with the winged things in the sky. Silas began to look again for once-familiar herbs. As her life unfolded, so did his soul.

By the time Eppie was three years old, she was finding ways to make mischief. Silas was puzzled about what to do. Dolly told him a spanking now and then was good for Eppie. "There's another thing you might do," Dolly added. "You might shut her up once in the coal hole. That's what I did with Aaron. I could never bear to smack him. The coal hole was as good as a spanking to him."

This troubled Silas. It was painful for him to hurt Eppie, and he feared that she might love him the less for it.

One morning, Silas had left his scissors within her reach. She cut the long linen band that held her to the loom. In moments, she had run out the open door into the sunshine. It was not until he needed the scissors that the terrible fact of her escape burst upon him.

Eppie had run out by herself. Perhaps she had fallen into the Stone Pits. Silas, shaken by fear, rushed out calling "Eppie!" At last he found her by a pond. She was talking cheerfully to her own boot, which she was using for a bucket.

Silas was overcome with joy. He covered her with kisses and carried her home. It was only then that he realized he needed to punish Eppie, to "make her remember." The idea that she might run away again gave him the strength of will to punish the child.

"Naughty, naughty Eppie," he began. "Naughty to cut with the scissors and run away. Daddy must put her in the coal hole."

He thought she would cry. Instead, she seemed pleased. He put her into the coal hole and held the door closed. After a moment came the cry, "Opy, opy." Silas let her out, saying, "Now, Eppie must be good, or she will go in the coal hole again." But the punishment did not work. Eppie came out of the hole covered in black dust. She loved the coal hole. It had been just another happy adventure for her.

In half an hour, she was clean again. Silas went back to work, thinking there was no need for the linen band for the rest of the morning. Some time later, he turned around again to place her in her little chair. She peeped out at him with black face and hands, and said, "Eppie in the coal hole!" Punishing her was clearly no use.

So Eppie was reared without punishment. "She'd take it all for fun," he told Dolly. "I'd have to hurt her, and that I can't do." Silas's stone cottage was made into a soft nest for Eppie. Silas took her on his journeys to the farmhouses. Eppie became an object of interest everywhere. Silas was no longer treated as a strange creature. Now he was met with open, smiling faces. No one was afraid of Silas when Eppie was near him. The little child had connected him once more with the outside world.

One person watched Eppie's growth with sharper interest than others, though it was hidden. He did not feel very bad about not being a father to his daughter. The child was being taken care of. She would likely be happy in her humble place.

Godfrey Cass's cheek and eye were brighter than ever now. Dunsey had not come back. People decided that he had left the country.

He imagined himself seated with happiness by his own fireplace. Nancy would smile at him as he played with their children. As for that other child, he would not forget it. He would see that it was well provided for. That was a father's duty.

9   Sixteen Years Later

It was a bright autumn Sunday. Sixteen years had passed since Silas Marner found his new treasure on his hearth. The bells of the old Raveloe church were ringing the end of the service.

Among those leaving the church were some we shall recognize. The tall, blond man of 40 has the same face as the Godfrey Cass of 26. He is only fuller in flesh. He no longer looks young. Perhaps the pretty woman leaning on his arm is more changed than her husband. Yet some people love faces best for what they tell of human experience. To them, Nancy's beauty is more interesting.

Mr. and Mrs. Cass turned around to show a tall, aged man and a plainly dressed woman. (The title "Squire" died with his father, when the Squire's lands were divided.) Nancy said they must wait for "Father and Priscilla." They all turned in on a path leading to the Red House. We will not follow them. There are others we want to see again.

It was impossible to mistake Silas Marner. His large brown eyes seem to have gained a longer sight. Otherwise, he has been weakened by 16 years. His shoulders are bent, and his hair is white.

But there is a fresh blossom by his side. It is a girl of 18. Little curls show themselves below her bonnet. Eppie is troubled by her hair. No other girl in Raveloe has hair like it. She thinks all hair ought to be smooth.

The young man behind Eppie likes her hair. She knows he is thinking about her and gathering his courage to come to her side.

"I wish we had a little garden, Father, like Mrs. Winthrop's," said Eppie. "Only it would take a good deal of digging. I shouldn't like you to do that. It would be too hard for you."

"Yes, I could do it, if you want a garden. Why didn't you tell me before that you wanted one?"

"I can dig it for you, Master Marner," said the young man. He was now by Eppie's side. "It would be fun for me. I can bring you some soil from Mr. Cass's garden—he'd let me."

"Eh, Aaron, my lad, are you there?" asked Silas. "Well, if you could help me, we might get her a bit of garden sooner."

"But only if you promise me you won't work at the hard digging, Father," said Eppie. "You and I can mark out the beds and plant the roots."

"I'll come to the Stone Pits this afternoon," said Aaron. "We'll decide where the garden shall be."

"Well, don't ask too much at Red House," Silas said. "Mr. Cass has been so good to us. He built up the new end of the cottage and gave us many things."

"Bring your mother with you, Aaron," Eppie said. "I want her to know everything about the garden."

Aaron turned back toward the village. Silas and Eppie went on toward the cottage.

Slowly, Silas had connected his new life and his old. He had first done this by opening his mind to Dolly Winthrop about his early life. Since Eppie had grown, Silas often talked with her, too, about the past. He told her how and why he had been alone until she had been sent to him.

Silas could not hide from Eppie that she was not his own child. She had long known how her mother had died. She knew she had been found on the hearth by Silas. He had given her the wedding ring that had been taken from her mother's thin finger. Eppie often looked at the ring, but she seldom thought about the father it suggested. Had she not a real father very close to her?

Who her mother was and how she had died was often on Eppie's mind. The bush against which she had died was still there. This afternoon, it was in her eyes and thoughts.

"Father, we shall take the bush into the garden," she said.

"Ah, child, it wouldn't do to leave out that bush," Silas said. "But we must have a fence. Else animals will come in and trample it all down."

"We could make a wall, Father," said Eppie. "We could use the stones from around the big pit. You and I could carry the smallest. Aaron would carry the rest." She skipped over to the pit. She meant to lift one of the stones and show her strength. "Oh, Father, come look!" she said. "See how the water's gone down since yesterday."

Silas came to her side. "Well, to be sure," he said. "Mr. Godfrey Cass has been draining it."

"How odd it will be to have the old pit dried up," Eppie said. She turned away. She and Silas sat on the stone bank in silence for a while. A tree threw happy, playful shadows all around them.

"Father," said Eppie, "if I marry, should I wear my mother's ring?"

"Why, Eppie, have you been thinking about marriage?" asked Silas in a low tone.

"Only this last week, Father," Eppie said, "since Aaron asked me. He's going on 24, and he has a lot of gardening work now."

"And you mean to have him, do you?" asked Silas.

"Yes, sometime," said Eppie. "Aaron says that everyone gets married sometime. But that's not true. Look at you, Father. You've never been married."

"No, child," said Silas. "Your father was a lone man till you were sent to him."

"But you'll never be lone again, Father," said Eppie. "Aaron wants us all to live together. You needn't work anymore. He'd be as good as a son to you. That's what he said."

"And should you like that, Eppie?" asked Silas, looking at her.

"I shouldn't mind it, Father," Eppie said. "I would like to go on for a long, long while just as we are. But Aaron does want a change."

"Eh, blessed child," said Silas. "You're young to be married. We'll ask Mrs. Winthrop. We'll ask Aaron's mother what she thinks. If there's a right thing to do, she'll say it. But think on this, Eppie. Things *will* change, whether we like it or not. I'll get older and be a burden on you. I'd like to think you'd have someone to take care of you."

"Then would you like me to be married?" asked Eppie.

"I won't say no," Silas said. "We'll ask your godmother. She'll wish the right thing by you and by her son, too."

"Here they come, then," Eppie said. "Let us go and meet them."

10 Secrets Revealed

While Silas and Eppie talked, Miss Priscilla Lammeter and her father were in the Red House. Nancy was inviting them to stay for tea. They were eating their dessert of fruit and nuts.

The dark parlor had changed since Godfrey's bachelor days. It was now all polish and order, thanks to Nancy.

"Now, Father, must you go home for tea?" Nancy asked. "Can't you stay with us? It's likely to be a beautiful evening."

"My dear, you must ask Priscilla," said the old gentleman. "She manages me and the farm, too."

"Then manage to stay for tea," said Nancy to her sister. "Come now. We'll go 'round the garden while Father has his nap."

"My dear child, he'll have a beautiful nap on the way home. I shall drive the carriage. But we can walk now, while the horse is being readied."

The sisters walked along the well-swept garden paths. "I'm glad that your husband is trading that land with Cousin Osgood," Priscilla said. "Now he can begin the dairy. It'll give you something to fill your mind. With a dairy, there's always something new to do."

"Ah, Priscilla, a dairy won't mean much to Godfrey," said Nancy. "I'm happy with the blessings we have. If only Godfrey could be happy."

"That's the way of men, always wanting and wanting, and never easy with what they've got."

"Don't say so, Priscilla," Nancy said. "Godfrey is the best of husbands. It's natural he should be disappointed at not having children. He always wanted them. There's many men would complain more than he does."

"Oh, I know," said Priscilla. "I know the way of wives, praising their husbands as if they wanted to sell them. But we must return. Father is waiting."

The carriage was at the front door. Mr. Lammeter was on the steps talking to Godfrey.

"Bring Nancy to our house before the week is out, Mr. Cass," said Priscilla as she took the reins.

"I shall just take a walk near the Stone Pits, Nancy," said Godfrey. "I want to look at the draining. I shall be back in an hour."

Godfrey often took a Sunday afternoon walk while he thought about his farming. Nancy seldom went with him. Women of her day did not often walk beyond their own garden—except those like Priscilla, who took to outdoor management. Nancy sat and read the Bible and let her thoughts wander.

Not many subjects took up Nancy's mind. She filled the time by living inside herself. She often thought about her past feelings and actions. There was one painful thought that she often visited. It was that Godfrey could never accept the absence of children from their life. Yet Nancy might have felt the absence even more. Wasn't there a drawer filled 14 years ago by the work of her hands? Only one little dress had been used. It had become the burial dress for their only child.

She always tried to think of everything as her husband saw it. Had she been right in resisting his wish to adopt a child? Adoption was not so often done or thought of in that time. Nancy did not believe in adopting a child because you could have none of your own. It was like going against God's will. The adopted child would never turn out well.

"But why should you think that?" Godfrey asked. "The child has done well with the weaver, and *he* adopted her."

"But he didn't go seeking her, as we would be doing," said Nancy. "It would be wrong, I'm sure. I know it's hard for you but it's God's will."

Godfrey had always spoken of Eppie as the child they should adopt. It never occurred to him that Silas might rather die than part with her. They were well off. They would be taking a charge off the hands of a poor man. Was that not right? Surely the weaver would wish the best for the child. He would be glad for her good luck.

"I was right to say no, even though it hurt me so!" Nancy thought. "Godfrey has never said an unkind word about it. It's only what he can't hide. Everything seems so blank to him. I see it when he looks after the farm. What a difference it would make to him to have children to be doing it for!"

Godfrey knew of his wife's loving effort to have children. It was impossible to have lived with her for fifteen years and to not have been aware of it. It also seemed impossible for him ever to tell the truth about Eppie. Nancy would be disgusted by the story of his earlier marriage. The very sight of Eppie would hurt her.

It had been four years since Godfrey had last discussed adopting Eppie. Nancy supposed it was forever buried.

That afternoon when Godfrey returned from the Stone Pits, he laid down his hat with trembling hands. He turned to Nancy with a pale face and a strange look in his eyes.

"I came back as soon as I could," he said. "I didn't want anybody to tell you but me. It's Dunstan—my brother who disappeared 16 years ago. We've found him—found his skeleton. The Stone Pits have gone dry from the draining. There he lies, stuck between two stones. There's his watch, and my hunting whip. He took it with him that last day he was seen."

"Do you think he drowned himself?" Nancy asked. She wondered why her husband should be so shaken by something that happened so long ago.

"No, he fell in," said Godfrey, quietly. Then he

added, "It was Dunstan who robbed Silas Marner."

"Oh, Godfrey!" Nancy said. She understood the shame he must have been feeling.

"The money was in the pit. It's been gathered up. They're taking the skeleton to the Rainbow. But I came back to tell you."

He was silent, looking at the ground. Nancy did not speak. She had a sense that Godfrey had something else to tell her.

Then he looked at her. "Everything comes to light, Nancy. When God wills it, our secrets are found out. I've lived with a secret, too, but I'll keep it from you no longer. I wouldn't have you find it out after I'm dead. Nancy, that woman Marner found dead in the snow—Eppie's mother. That wretched woman was my wife. Eppie is my child."

Nancy sat as pale and quiet as a statue.

"You'll never think the same of me again," said Godfrey. "I shouldn't have left the child. I shouldn't have kept it from you. But I couldn't bear to give you up, Nancy."

Nancy remained silent. He expected she would leave him now. How could she forgive him? But at last she looked at him and spoke. There was no anger in her voice, only regret.

"Godfrey, if you had told me this before, we could have done right by the child. Do you think I would have refused to take her in, knowing she was yours? She'd have loved me for her mother. I could have better stood my little baby dying. Our life could have been like we wanted it to be. I wasn't worth doing wrong for. Nothing is."

"I'm a worse man than you ever thought I was," Godfrey said. "Can you forgive me, ever?"

"The wrong to me is little, Godfrey. You've been good to me for 15 years. It's someone else you did the wrong to. I doubt you could ever make it up."

"But we can take Eppie now," Godfrey said. "I won't mind the world knowing at last."

"It will be different, now that she's grown up," Nancy said. "But it's your duty to acknowledge her and provide for her. I'll do my part by her, too."

"We'll go together to Marner's tonight," said Godfrey.

11 Eppie's Choice

That evening, Eppie and Silas were alone in the cottage. After the excitement of that afternoon, Silas had longed for quiet. Now he sat in his armchair and looked at Eppie. On the table lay his old, long-loved gold. It was arranged in neat piles, as in the days when it was his only joy. He told her how he used to count it every night and how empty he had been before she was sent to him.

"If you hadn't been sent to save me, I should have gone to the grave in my misery," he said. "The money was taken from me. You see it's been kept till it was wanted for you. It's wonderful. Our life is wonderful."

Silas sat looking at the money. "It takes no hold of me now," he said. "It might again, if I lost you, Eppie. I might come to think I was lost again and lose the feeling that God was good to me."

There was a knock at the door. Eppie opened it. She saw Mr. and Mrs. Godfrey Cass. She made a little curtsey and held the door open for them.

"We're disturbing you very late, my dear," said Mrs. Cass. She took Eppie's hand. Eppie was nervous. She placed chairs for Mr. and Mrs. Cass. Then she stood beside Silas, facing them.

"Well, Marner," Godfrey tried to speak firmly. "It's a great comfort to see you with your money again. It was one of my family that did you wrong. I feel bound to make up for it in every way. But there are other things I owe you for, Marner."

Silas was always ill at ease when spoken to by his "betters." "Sir, I have much to thank you for already," Silas said. "As for the robbery, I count it no loss to me. Even if I did, it wasn't your fault."

"You may look at it that way, Marner, but I hope you'll let me do what I think is just. I know you've always worked hard," said Godfrey.

"Yes," said Silas. "Work was what I held by when everything else was gone from me."

"Well, weaving was a good trade for you. There's always a need for it. But you're getting rather past such hard work, Marner. It's time you had some rest. You've done a good part by Eppie. It would be a great comfort to you to see her well provided for, wouldn't it? You'd like to see her taken care of by those who can leave her well off. She's more fit to be a lady than for a rough life."

"I don't take your meaning sir," Silas said. He was feeling hurt and uneasy. He did not have the words to express what he felt.

"Well, my meaning is this," said Godfrey. "Mrs. Cass and I, you know, have no children.

"We should like to have Eppie in the place of a daughter to us. We would treat her as our own child in every way. It would be a comfort for you, I hope, to see her fortune made that way. Eppie, I'm sure, will always love you and be grateful to you. She'd come to see you often. And we'd do anything we could to make you comfortable," explained Godfrey.

A plain man like Godfrey Cass can blunder on his words. They can be hard on people's feelings. Eppie felt Silas tremble violently. She was about to say something. Then, at last, Silas said, faintly:

"Eppie, my child, speak. I won't stand in your way. Thank Mr. and Mrs. Cass."

Eppie came forward. Her cheeks were flushed, but not with shyness. "Thank you, ma'am—thank you, sir," she said. "But I can't leave my father. There's no one dearer to me. And I don't want to be a lady— thank you all the same. I couldn't give up the folks I'm used to."

Godfrey only thought of reclaiming Eppie. He had not expected this answer. He spoke with anger. "But I have a claim on you, Eppie. It is my duty, Marner, to own Eppie as my child, and to provide for her. She is my own child. Her mother was my wife."

Eppie gave a violent start. She turned pale. Silas, however, felt freed by Eppie's answer.

"Then, sir, why didn't you say so 16 years ago?" Silas asked. The bitterness he had long kept silent was in his voice. "Why didn't you say so before I'd come to love her? You might as well take the heart out of my body. God gave her to me because you turned your back on her. He looks upon her as mine. You've no right to her!"

"I know that, Marner. I was wrong. I've been sorry about how I behaved."

"I am glad to hear it, sir," Marner said, "but it doesn't change what's been going on for 16 years. It's me she's been calling 'Father' ever since she could say the word."

"But I think you might be more reasonable," said Godfrey. "It isn't as if you'd never see her again. She'll feel just the same toward you."

"Just the same as now when we drink of the same cup? That's idle talk. You'd cut us in two," replied Silas.

"I should have thought you'd be happy in what was best for Eppie," Godfrey said. "So what if you do have to give up something? She might marry some low working man. Then what could I do for her? You're putting yourself in the way of her good fortune. I'm sorry to hurt you, but I feel I must insist on taking care of my own daughter."

Eppie's mind raced as she listened. Now Eppie felt only revulsion to this newly revealed father and what he offered.

"I'll say no more," said Silas. "Speak to the child. Let her decide."

"Eppie, my dear," Godfrey began, "I haven't been

to you what a father should be. But I wish to do everything I can for you for the rest of my life. And you'll have the best of mothers in my wife."

"My dear, you'll be a treasure to me," said Nancy in her gentle voice. Even she did not think Silas was reasonable in wanting to keep Eppie.

Eppie held Silas's hand. She spoke more coldly than before. "Thank you for your offers," she said. "They're far above my wish. I've got but one father. I'll stay with him as long as he lives. He's cared for me and loved me from the first."

"But you must be sure, Eppie," Silas said. "You've made your choice to stay among poor folks. You might have had everything of the best."

"I can never be sorry, Father," Eppie said, while the tears gathered. "I can't think of another home. I shouldn't know what to do with fine things. It would be poor work for me to make those I love think I'm too good for them. I like the working folks and their houses and their ways. And I've promised to marry a working man. He'll live with Father and help me take care of him."

Godfrey looked at Nancy. Both knew they had lost their last hope for a child. "Let us go," he said quietly.

"We won't talk of this any longer now," said Nancy. "We wish you well. We shall come and see you again. It's getting late." In this way she covered her husband's quick exit. Godfrey had gone straight to the door, unable to say more.

"Well, perhaps it isn't too late to mend a bit there," Godfrey said later that night. "Though it *is* too late to mend some things."

12 The Return

The next morning, Silas and Eppie were seated at breakfast. "Eppie, there's a thing I've had on my mind to do," he said. "Now that my money has been brought back, we can do it. We'll make a little bundle of things and set out tomorrow."

"To go where, Father?" asked Eppie, surprised.

"To my old country—to the town where I was born. Something may have come out to show them I was innocent of the robbery."

Four days later, Silas and Eppie were walking through a great manufacturing town. Silas was confused by the changes that 30 years had brought to it. He stopped several people to ask the name of the town, to be sure he had not made a mistake.

"Ask for Lantern Yard, Father," Eppie said. "Ask this gentleman standing in the shop door."

"He won't know," said Silas. "Gentlefolk never went up to the Yard. But maybe somebody can show me Prison Street, where the jail is. I'd know my way out of there as if I'd seen it yesterday."

After many questions, they finally found their way to the streets Silas remembered. "Oh, Father, it's like I can't breathe!" said Eppie. "I couldn't have thought folks lived this way, so close together."

"It looks funny to me, child, now. It smells bad, too. I can't think it used to smell so."

They reached the entry to Lantern Yard. "Dear heart!" Silas said. "Why, there's people coming out of the Yard as if they'd been to chapel—on a weekday noon!"

Suddenly, Silas stood still. They were standing in front of a large factory. Men and women were streaming out of it for their midday meal.

"Father, what's the matter?" Eppie said.

"It's gone, child," he said at last. He was very upset. "Lantern Yard's gone. It must have been here. I remember this house. See that big factory! It's all gone—chapel and all!"

No one they talked to knew anything of the former town or people of Lantern Yard.

"The old place is all swept away," Silas said to Dolly Winthrop on their return to Raveloe. "I shall never know whether they discovered the real truth of the robbery. It's dark to me. I don't doubt it will be dark to the last."

"Well, yes, Master Marner," said Dolly. "Many things are dark to us. It's the will of Them above. It seems that you'll never know the rights of it. But that doesn't keep there from *being* a rights of it."

"No," said Silas. "No, it doesn't. The child was sent to me, and I've come to love her. I've had enough light to trust by. I think I shall trust now till I die."

The sunshine fell warmly on the flowers the morning Eppie was married. Her dress was pure white. Mrs. Godfrey Cass had begged to provide it. Eppie walked across the churchyard and down to the village. One hand was on her husband's arm. With the other, she clasped Silas's hand. Dolly Winthrop walked behind with her husband.

Many eyes watched the wedding procession. Miss Priscilla Lammeter and her father were at the Red House. They were keeping Nancy company. Mr. Cass had had to go away. That was a pity. He would miss the wedding feast he had ordered at the Rainbow. The guests talked of Silas Marner's strange history. They agreed that he had brought a blessing on himself by acting as a father to Eppie.

The wedding party continued on to the Stone Pits. There had been changes there. At the expense of Mr. Cass, the cottage had been enlarged to suit Silas's larger family. For he and Eppie had declared that they would rather stay there than go to any new home.

"Oh, Father!" said Eppie. "I think nobody could be happier than we are."